This Book Belongs to:

Mickey's Young Readers Library

VOLUME

6

Mickey's Magic Bottle

STORY BY DIANE NAMM

Activities by Thoburn Educational Enterprises, Inc.

A BANTAM BOOK
NEW YORK · TORONTO · LONDON · SYDNEY · AUCKLAND

Mickey's Magic Bottle   A Bantam Book/September 1990. All rights reserved. © 1990 The Walt Disney Company. Developed by
The Walt Disney Company in conjunction with Nancy Hall, Inc. This book may not be reproduced or transmitted in any form or by any means.
ISBN 0–553–05619–0
Published simultaneously in the United States and Canada. Bantam Books are published by Bantam Doubleday Dell Publishing Group,
Inc. Its trademark, consisting of the words "Bantam Books" and the portrayal of a rooster, is Registered in U.S. Patent
and Trademark Office and in other countries. Marca Registrada. Bantam Books 666 Fifth Avenue, New York, New York 10103.
Printed in the United States of America
0 9 8 7 6 5 4 3 2 1
A Walt Disney BOOK FOR YOUNG READERS

One day, Goofy and Donald went to visit Mickey. Mickey was staying at his grandfather's house while his grandfather was away.

"Hello there, Mickey," Goofy called from the doorway.

"Oh, hi, fellas," Mickey replied. "Gee, I'm glad to see you two. I have a really big favor to ask."

"What's up?" Donald wanted to know.

Mickey held up a dusty, old bottle. "I have to go to the store to get some things before my grandfather returns. But I need someone to watch the bottle while I'm out."

"Gawrsh, Mickey, why does a bottle need a baby-sitter?" Goofy asked.

"Well, last night, when I was cleaning out the basement, I found this old bottle. I began to shine it with a cloth. But when I rubbed it—a genie popped out! And he told me he would grant me three wishes!"

"Gawrsh, Mickey—are you joking?" Goofy asked.

"No, really—it's true!" Mickey replied. "But I can't decide what my three wishes should be. And I need someone to watch the bottle until I know what to ask the genie. So what do you say, fellas? Will you do it?" Mickey asked.

"Gawrsh, Mickey, I don't know about this genie stuff," Goofy began to say.

But Donald's eyes had opened wide when he heard that the genie would grant Mickey three wishes. He hushed Goofy and said, "Why, sure, Mickey. We'll be glad to help you out."

"Thanks," Mickey said, handing over the bottle.
Then he left, promising to return as soon as he could.

No sooner was Mickey out the door than
Donald and Goofy looked at the bottle closely.
"It looks like a plain old bottle to me," Goofy
said.
"That's because we haven't rubbed it yet, like
Mickey said," Donald told him.
"Do you think we should?" Goofy asked.
"Why not?" Donald replied. "Mickey won't mind.

He'll get to ask for his three wishes when he gets back. While he's gone, we can ask the genie to grant some wishes for us!" Donald smiled at the thought of all the things that he might wish for. He hummed happily to himself as he looked around for something with which to rub the bottle.

"Aha! This will do just fine," Donald said, holding up an old cloth.

"I'm not so sure I want to meet this genie, Donald," Goofy started to say. But before Goofy could say another word, Donald rubbed the bottle.

Suddenly, a big cloud of purple smoke appeared above them!

When the smoke had cleared, a large genie stood before them. With a twinkle in his eye, the genie said, "Good day, my friends. Make three wishes, and I'll be happy to grant them."

Both Donald's and Goofy's eyes opened wide.

"Gawrsh, a real, live genie!" was all Goofy could say.

"W-w-w-will you grant us *both* three wishes?" Donald asked.

"I will grant you each one wish, and the third you must share," the genie replied. "Nothing more, nothing less. And be careful, my friends. What you wish for is what you'll get!" he added with a grin.

Then he disappeared back into the bottle.

Donald rubbed his hands together with glee.
"Oh, boy! Three wishes. What should I wish for?"
"Remember, Donald, one of those wishes is
mine, and one we have to share!" Goofy said.
"Yes, yes, I know. Now, what should we wish for
first? Cars? Houses? Money?" Donald couldn't
decide what he wanted most.

Goofy scratched his head. He thought and thought. "Gee, Donald, you know—all this thinking is making me kind of hungry. I wonder if Mickey has anything to eat around here."

Donald was so busy thinking about his wish, that he didn't hear what Goofy had said.

Goofy looked around. There wasn't any food to be found. Without thinking he said out loud, "I wish we had a fine turkey dinner right now!"

No sooner did the words leave Goofy's mouth than a turkey dinner appeared on the table.

"Gawrsh, how did that get here?" Goofy asked.

Donald just stared at the table full of food.

"Oh, Goofy! What did you just say?"

Goofy told him.

"How could you waste one of our wishes on food?" Donald moaned.

"Well, golly, Donald, I didn't mean to do it,"
Goofy explained. "The words just slipped right out!
Besides, it was *my* wish I wasted—not yours. You still
have one, and we still have one together," Goofy
added.

"But, we could have wished for enough food for a year!" Donald sputtered. "You know, Goofy, you make me so angry! I wish that drumstick was stuck to your nose!"

Then Donald covered his mouth with a cry.

For, of course, no sooner had he made his foolish wish, than the drumstick appeared at the end of Goofy's nose!

"Oh, no! I take it back. I didn't mean it," Donald said to the magic bottle.

But the drumstick stayed stuck.

"This is just great, Donald," Goofy said. "How are we going to get this drumstick off my nose?"

"Let's try pulling it off. Maybe it isn't stuck for good," Donald hoped.

Donald tugged and tugged. Goofy pulled and pulled. They tugged and pulled until Goofy's nose was sore. But the drumstick would not come unstuck!

Donald sat down beside Goofy. "Two wishes wasted!" was all he could say.

"How can you think about nothing but those three silly wishes at a time like this!" Goofy cried. Then he thought for a minute.

"That's it!" Goofy said happily. "We have one more wish. We can use that to take the drumstick off my nose!"

"Oh, no you don't!" Donald told him. "We're not wasting our very last wish on your nose! We'll think of something else!" Donald looked around the room, looking for something to help unstick the drumstick.

"I've got it!" Donald said with great excitement.
"Let's call back the genie. We'll tell him it was all a
big mistake. He'll understand that we didn't mean
those two silly wishes. I bet he'll give us two more.
He seemed like a nice genie!" Donald said.

Goofy rubbed his poor nose. He was not so sure. "He didn't seem all that nice to me," Goofy said in a low voice.

But Donald wasn't listening. He ran over to the bottle and rubbed it as hard as he could. In a flash, the purple cloud of smoke appeared, and the grinning genie stood before them.

"Two wishes wished. Two wishes received. Tell me, friends, what will your last wish be?" the genie asked them. His eyes twinkled as he stared at the drumstick stuck to Goofy's nose.

"That's just what we want to talk to you about," Donald began. "You know, we haven't had much practice at making wishes, and, I mean . . . those first two don't really count, do they? After all, we didn't mean what we said," he explained.

"I'm sorry," the genie replied, "but magic is a funny thing. As I told you in the beginning, what you wished for is what you would get. Your last wish together is all you have left!" Then he disappeared. Donald and Goofy heard a deep laugh from inside the bottle.

Donald stared sadly at the bottle.

"I guess you're right, Goofy. The only way we're going to unstick that drumstick is to use up our very last wish. Our one and only chance for cars, houses, and money!" Donald said. Then he added, "Unless you could learn to live with a drumstick on your nose. You know, it doesn't really look that bad . . ." Donald started to say.

"Aw, come on, Donald. You don't really want me to spend the rest of my life with a drumstick on my nose!" Goofy said.

"You're right, Goofy. Let's just make the last wish and get it over with," Donald said with a sigh.

Then they both closed their eyes and wished that the drumstick would disappear from Goofy's nose.

When they opened their eyes, the drumstick was back on the plate where it belonged. Donald looked sadly at the turkey. Goofy patted his nose, which felt as good as new.

"Cheer up, Donald—things aren't all that bad," Goofy said. "At least we still have this fine turkey dinner."

But Donald was much too unhappy to answer,
or to eat. He just stared off into space, thinking of all
the things he could have wished for and hadn't.

After awhile, Mickey returned. He stared with wonder at all the food on the table.

But before Mickey could ask what had happened, Donald picked up the magic bottle and pushed it into Mickey's arms.

"Here, take your magic bottle. Make your three silly wishes. I hope I never see this bottle again as long as I live!" Donald said. Then he left in a huff.

"What's wrong with him?" Mickey asked.

"Aw, what he really meant to say was you have to watch what you wish for," Goofy said between bites.

"Why is that?" asked Mickey.

"Because what you wish may turn out to be exactly what you get!" added a deep voice from the bottle.

Think About It

What Comes Next?

For each group of sentences, point to the picture that shows what happened next in the story.

1. Mickey asked Donald and Goofy to watch his magic bottle. While Mickey was gone, Donald suggested they call for the genie in the bottle.

2. Donald didn't know what his wish should be. While they were deciding, Goofy got hungry and wished for something to eat.

3. Donald got very angry at Goofy for his silly wish. But then Donald made a silly wish of his own!

After your child does the activities in this book, refer to the *Young Readers Guide* for the answers to these activities and for additional games, activities, and ideas.

Make-A-Wish

What were some of the things that Donald
wanted to wish for? What would your three wishes
be if you had a magic bottle like Mickey's?

Fun With Words

Match-A-Word

Point to the word that best describes each picture.

1. stuck

2. unstuck

3. unhappy

4. happy

a.

b.

c.

d.

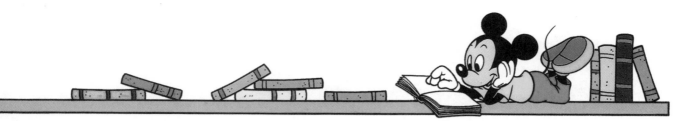

The Genie's Message

See if you can find the three opposite pairs of words in the genie's message.

The secret of the magic bottle is this: Be careful what wish you've made, it cannot be unmade. When you rub the bottle, I appear. But once I've explained my powers, I will disappear at once. I have the power to make you the happiest person or the unhappiest person in the world. And now, my friends, the rest is up to you!